UNDERWEAR

What We Wear Under There

by Ruth Freeman Swain

illustrated by John O'Brien

DONATIONS

Holiday House / New York

To Sarah
R. F. S.

For Tess
J. O.

Text copyright © 2008 by Ruth Freeman Swain
Illustrations copyright © 2008 by John O'Brien
All Rights Reserved
Printed and Bound in China
The text typeface is Olduval.
The illustrations were done in watercolor over ink on Strathmore Bristol paper.
www.holidayhouse.com
First Edition
1 3 5 7 9 10 8 6 4 2

Library of Congress Cataloging-in-Publication Data
Swain, Ruth Freeman.
Underwear : what we wear under there / by Ruth Freeman Swain ;
illustrated by John O'Brien. — 1st ed.
p. cm.
ISBN 978-0-8234-1920-3 (hardcover)
1. Underwear—History—Juvenile literature.
I. O'Brien, John, 1953– ill. II. Title.
GT2073.S93 2008
391.4'2—dc22
2008004041

People have giggled about it, snickered about it, and whispered about it (shhh) for hundreds of years. They've made jokes; they've teased. They've been too embarrassed to talk about it out loud, even though they have a pretty good idea what's under there.

What is it? What is so funny about underwear?

The earliest people didn't have a whole lot of time for any underwear at all. They were too busy trying to survive. But as they moved to cooler climates, and when they wanted to keep their private parts private, the simplest, easiest answer was the breechclout. A breechclout, or breechcloth, is a strip of leather worn between the legs and looped over a cord tied around the waist. Many Native Americans wore breechclouts, including the Wampanoag in Massachusetts when the Pilgrims landed.

After people learned how to weave cloth, loincloths became the earliest form of underpants. A single strip of fabric could be wrapped around the waist and through the legs, and tucked in. Loincloths were worn in all parts of the ancient world, from the Incas to the Romans, from Africa to China. Though most people didn't pose for paintings in their underwear, Egyptian men are shown in ancient tomb paintings wearing linen loincloths called *"schentis"* that look like little skirts.

In India men still wear large cotton loincloths called *"dhotis."* Mahatma Gandhi, one of the most famous people in India, was often photographed wearing a simple white dhoti as he worked for a new and independent India.

During the Middle Ages in Europe, women wore coarse shifts over their loincloths for warmth. Men put on long shirts of scratchy wool or rough linen. Men also added leggings like those originally worn by early Germanic tribes fighting the Romans. (The Romans ended up stealing the tribes' ideas for pants as well as their lands.) By the fifteenth century men's leggings became so tight they looked like stockings. Worn under very short jackets, or doublets, the leggings were often two different colors or striped. But one thing these fancy leggings could not do was stretch, because they were cut and sewn from cloth. Perhaps that is why well-dressed men of the period are often painted standing up. At any rate men and boys continued to show off their legs for the next four hundred years.

Knights in fifteenth-century Europe wore special padded underwear in order to protect their bodies from their suits of plate armor. Quilted leggings and padded arming doublets were worn. An arming doublet had straps that tied pieces of armor onto it. All clothing had to be tied, pinned, or laced together since there were no zippers, no snaps, and no Velcro!

At about the same time, in Japan warriors were known as samurai. Each one was trained to serve his lord with absolute loyalty and to show no fear in battle. Under a skirted tunic sewn with iron scales, baggy trousers, and a kimono, the samurai wore a *"fundoshi,"* the traditional loincloth. When there was trouble a warrior would tighten his fundoshi to help him concentrate. Today sumo wrestlers still wear a heavier and thicker type of fundoshi.

There is an old saying, "Don't air your dirty linen in public," meaning, don't spread private, unpleasant details about yourself for everyone to hear. Well, underwear in sixteenth-century England was the original "dirty linen." Shirts and shifts were gray with dirt and smelled of sweat. Underwear was alive with fleas, ticks, and mites because people rarely took baths. But underwear had an important job to do: It protected people's better outer clothes, which were hard to wash, from the dirt and smells of their bodies. It was easier to wash underwear—at least a few times a year.

The linen shirts of Henry VIII (1491–1547), king of England, may not have been the cleanest; but they looked very fine with their gold thread and lace. Shirts were still thought of as underwear but not for much longer. It was the fashion for men to wear doublets and sleeves with fancy slashes with shirts poking through. Underwear sometimes became outerwear.

Henry's daughter Elizabeth I (1533–1603), queen of England, loved fine clothes as much as her father did. During her years as queen, one new women's fashion was possible only because of the construction worn underneath. The "farthingale" was a petticoat stiffened with hoops of wood or whalebone that held a dress from the body like a dome. Sometimes a cushion, shaped like a giant doughnut, was tied around the waist to hold the skirt out even more. This cushion was commonly called a "bum roll."

Though hooped petticoats changed in size and shape, they continued to be worn in eighteenth-century Europe and America. In the middle of the century, they grew flat in front and back, but they were sometimes as wide as six feet across at the sides. (Imagine holding a yardstick out on either side of you!) Called "panniers" from the French word for "basket," they made a woman look as if she had a basket on each hip. Doorways were difficult, carriages were a problem, and sitting in an armchair was impossible. Thank goodness collapsible, hinged panniers were designed so women could fold them up and sit down once in a while.

Toward the end of the century, young girls began wearing pantalettes under their dresses. Trimmed with lace or ruffles, pantalettes were meant to be seen below the shorter dresses. Each leg was separate from the other and only joined at the waist with drawstrings. Pantalettes would slowly shrink to become "drawers" in the next century, then "bloomers," and finally women's underpants today.

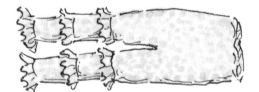 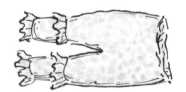 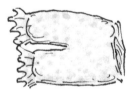

Fashions are often not designed for the natural shape of the human body. In nineteenth-century England and France, women learned to live with bodies tightly bound in corsets to have the small, slender waists required by society. Even men and boys sometimes wore corsets. People thought good posture was important for that straight-laced, upstanding, self-disciplined look. Many people also felt women needed extra support—a lot of it.

Tightly laced corsets could change a woman's body permanently by altering the position of her internal organs. With her lungs compressed she could take only short, shallow breaths. Unused muscles in her back and stomach grew so weak that, in time, it was uncomfortable to go without a corset. Digestion and childbearing could also be difficult.

At the same time that women wore corsets, they were dragging around huge skirts held out by as many as six starched petticoats. The layers were so hot and heavy that when the new cage crinoline arrived in 1856, women jumped into them. The crinoline was a petticoat stiffened with a cage of whalebone or steel hoops. Suddenly lighter without all those extra petticoats, the skirts grew even wider. They grew so wide that a skirt could measure six feet across on the floor, the size of a child's wading pool today!

Moving anywhere in a crinoline required great skill and constant attention. Girls learned to float gracefully down a staircase without ever seeing the steps beneath them, to sit without having their hoops fly up, and to get into a carriage without showing an ankle. There was a danger of fire if skirts swept too close to an open hearth. And there was the problem of wind . . . underpants, or drawers, were needed now more than ever before.

A few women decided they could do very well without corsets and crinolines. In 1851 in Seneca Falls, New York, a magazine editor, Amelia Bloomer, published a new idea from her friend Elizabeth Smith Miller. The idea was to wear a comfortable tunic over pajama-style pants. Amelia and her friends, who supported women's rights, were free to go on a hike, jump over a fence, even work in the garden! But people were horrified by the sight of women wearing pants. They teased and laughed at the women; children threw snowballs and apple cores at them. Years later, however, "bloomers" reappeared as part of women's bathing suits and bicycle outfits.

Other ideas were also changing the way people dressed in the nineteenth century. In 1864, when Louis Pasteur discovered microbes, or germs, and proved that they cause disease, people became very health-conscious. Many theories for staying healthy circulated, some more scientific than others. In the 1870s Dr. Gustav Jaeger of Germany believed everyone should wear his Sanitary Woolen System for good health. He claimed his knit underwear would hold in the body's warmth but let the "noxious exhalations of the body" (bad smells) out. Dr. Jaeger convinced so many people to wear his thick, scratchy "woolies" in winter and summer that he made a fortune selling underwear.

Woolen "combinations" in England were called "union suits" in the United States. They were a knitted top (soon to become the sweater) "united" to long woolen leggings to make one suit. Some suits came with drop seats, some came in a very popular scarlet red. In 1895 miners, lumberjacks, and whole farm families could order suits from the Montgomery Ward catalog for about a dollar each. At last, underwear came in the mail "ready-made" instead of it having to be made at home as people had done in the past.

The bottom half of a union suit got the name "long johns" from John L. Sullivan, an American bare-knuckles boxing champion of the 1880s and 1890s. Besides being a prizewinning boxer, he was known for fighting in his long underwear.

As the nineteenth century ended and the twentieth century began, the fashionable "S-bend" corset molded a woman's front into a fashionably large bosom, pinched her waist, and pushed her hips back into an unnatural curve. But the end of the corset was coming.

Women discovered bike riding in 1895 and the joy of getting around on their own. By 1900 more than four million women in America were working outside the home. Then in 1911 came the tango, from Argentina. It was all the rage. Women wanted to work, they wanted to play tennis, they wanted to dance.

Shorter, more flexible "bust supporters" became more popular than rigid corsets. Bust supporters led to brassieres, or "bras," which showed for the first time in years that a woman's chest was not one large "monobosom" after all.

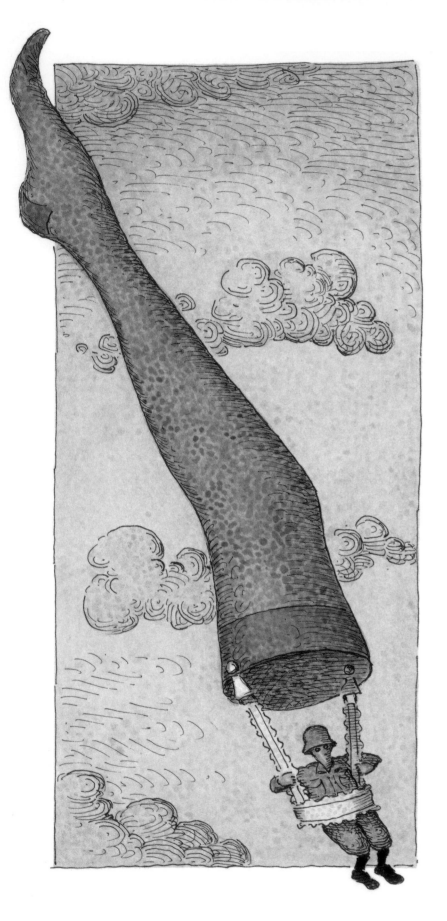

As hemlines rose in the 1920s and 1930s, silk stockings were very popular. But by the late 1930s, getting silk was a problem. Japan controlled the Chinese silk market; and in the years leading to World War II, relations between the United States and Japan became more strained.

In 1939 the DuPont company came up with the answer. At the New York World's Fair that year, they introduced a man-made silk called "nylon," the world's first synthetic fiber.

Nylon had only just gotten its name. DuPont scientists tried out more than four hundred names, including "Duparooh," from "DuPont Pulls a Rabbit Out of Hat." They wanted people to think nylon was like a magic trick because it came from the same elements in coal, air, and water. Other rejected names were "klis" ("silk" spelled backward) and "norun," since nylon stockings didn't run as easily as silk. It was "norun" that led finally to "nylon."

"N" Day was May 15, 1940, the day when nylon stockings first went on sale to the public. Across the country crowds waited for hours outside stores. Even though each customer could buy only one pair, three quarters of a million pairs of nylons sold out at once.

DuPont made nylons until the Japanese attacked Pearl Harbor in 1941, and the United States entered World War II. Then nylon was used to make parachutes, tents, and tires for B-29 bombers instead of stockings. Women who didn't want to be seen without their nylons drew lines up the backs of their legs. The lines looked like the seams running up the back of the kind of nylon stockings worn in the 1940s.

In the 1950s and 1960s, underwear became lighter and more comfortable. Much of it was made with younger people in mind. American teenage girls wore bobby socks, then pantyhose, when skirts shrank to minilengths. Teenage boys wore T-shirts with the sleeves rolled up, the way actors did in movies. Before the T-shirt became cool to wear, it was a plain undershirt, the top half of a man's summer union suit.

Luckily most families now had their own washers and dryers. For parents with babies in cloth diapers, these machines were great time-saving inventions. By the 1960s parents could also buy disposable diapers. Disposable diapers are popular today not only for babies but for adults—such as astronauts—as well!

Under the space suits that astronauts wear for launch, reentry, and space walks, they wear long underwear and adult diapers. At those times it just isn't possible to get to a toilet. Astronaut R. Mike Mullane once had to wait four hours for his space shuttle to take off. He said he remembers "lying in a very wet diaper, knowing why babies cry when they have wet diapers. It's gross!"

In earlier times and in other places, people have used whatever was clean and handy for diapers. Native Americans such as the Penobscot in Maine used soft, absorbent sphagnum moss. The Lenape in the Mid-Atlantic states used fine shredded cedar bark. In India and Nepal babies in rural areas are still diapered with pieces of worn cotton saris. And in hot African countries such as Ghana and Malawi, babies may wear nothing at all but are washed frequently in basins of water warmed by the sun.

Even though the climate in China is much cooler than in Malawi or Ghana, Chinese toddlers could skip wearing diapers too. It was the custom in China to dress young children in pants that were open at the crotch. The pants opened easily when needed and closed when children stood up. What a good idea!

In stores today underwear for children is cheap and easy to buy in all shapes, sizes, and fun colors. Briefs come with superheroes and favorite cartoon characters printed on them. When a pair of briefs is outgrown, it's easy to buy more in a bigger size.

But did you ever wonder what happens to an old pair of underpants? When used clothing, including underwear, is given to a place such as Goodwill Industries, underpants are recycled and begin a whole new life.

Instead of going into a landfill, the used clothing may be sold at a Goodwill store, or sold to a recycling company that converts it back into cotton fibers to be used in new ways, such as stuffing for dolls. Used clothes are also shipped in large bales to countries such as Zambia in Africa.

There, in open-air markets, people make a living selling secondhand clothes to buyers who are happy to find clothes they like at a cheap price. American fashions are very popular, even if buyers have never seen a cartoon or heard of a superhero.

Tomorrow's underwear may knock your socks off—but at least it will smell good. Researchers are working hard to invent new fabrics that will absorb perspiration and take it away from the body, a process they call "moisture management." Fabrics may also be treated to kill germs and deodorize smells so that underwear could be worn for a month without being washed! T-shirt fabric containing tiny ceramic particles is being tested to see if it will block harmful rays from the sun. A person wearing such a shirt will feel five degrees cooler than if he or she were wearing a normal shirt.

Will underwear still be funny in the future? Maybe it always will be. There's just something about it. Is it because underwear is usually hidden? Because it's the layer between being dressed and undressed? Because it's colorful, silly, skimpy, or just because it's . . . *under there*?

Can you say it in a whisper? Can you say it out loud? Can you say it without a smile?

"I see London,

I see France,

I see Laura's under_____!"

A BRIEF HISTORY OF UNDERWEAR

Ancient times	The earliest people wear breechclouts and loincloths.
Middle Ages	In Europe men wear shirts; women wear shifts (basically the same garment).
15th century	In Europe men wear tight-fitting leggings, or hose; arming doublets; and quilted leggings.
	In Japan, fundoshi are the traditional loincloths of samurai.
1491–1547	Henry VIII of England wears the latest fashion in underwear vs. outerwear. His shirt peeks through elaborate slashes in his doublet.
1533–1603	Elizabeth I of England and noble ladies wear farthingales and bum rolls under their dresses.
16th century	In Europe women begin wearing stiff "bodies," also called "stays" or "corsets," under their dresses.
18th century	In Europe and America women wear panniers under dresses. Toward the end of the century, girls wear pantalettes.
1828	Metal eyelets are invented that allow tighter lacing on corsets.
1851	Amelia Bloomer publishes a more rational idea for women's clothing: a comfortable tunic worn over pants. She was ahead of her time.
1856	The cage crinoline, a petticoat stiffened with a cage of whalebone hoops, arrives. Because whalebone was in great demand for the "bones" in underwear, many thousands of whales were killed for the bristly plates of baleen in their mouths. Many whales use baleen to filter fish and plankton from the ocean. Baleen was stronger, lighter, and more flexible than anything else until steel was used.
1864	Louis Pasteur proves diseases are caused by microbes, or germs. Before this time, people thought diseases and even new life came from rotten or nasty odors in the air. One seventeenth-century Belgian doctor, Jean Baptiste van Helmont, claimed he could grow mice in a jar from nothing but a few grains of wheat and a piece of stinky underwear!
1870s	Dr. Gustav Jaeger of Germany sells his Sanitary Woolen System underwear. A new emphasis on health and cleanliness begins.

1895   Montgomery Ward catalog advertises red woolen union suits for one dollar. Also called "long johns" after the boxer John L. Sullivan, who wore his long underwear in the ring.
The new passion for bicycle-riding requires shorter, more flexible corsets for women.

1900   The new S-bend, or straight-front, corset comes into fashion and is popularized in magazines as the Gibson Girl look. With the chest pushed forward, the back arched, and the hips thrown back at an unnatural angle, this new style corset was even more uncomfortable than earlier corsets.

1920s   Curves are out, a woman's ideal figure is now slender and straight.
Women use bust minimizers, binders, and bust flatteners.
With their shorter dresses, women begin wearing silk stockings.

1931   Lastex, a fabric made from rubber, is invented. The world of two-way stretch has arrived, Girdles are now called "roll-ons."

1939   The DuPont company introduces nylon, the world's first synthetic fiber, at the New York World's Fair. Another exhibit at the fair shows off something called "television."

1940   On May 15, "N" Day, 750,000 pairs of nylon stockings are sold.

1946   The United States tests an atom bomb on the Bikini Atoll, a chain of coral islands in the Pacific. At the same time, a French designer, Louis Reard, needed a name for his tiny new swimsuit. Figuring his design of four cloth triangles tied together with string was "explosive," he called it a "bikini." The name was soon used for underwear as it got smaller and smaller.

1950s   Teenage girls wear bobby socks; boys wear white T-shirts.

1959   Spandex, a synthetic elastic fiber, is invented. Also called "Lycra," it revolutionizes underwear.

1960s   Pantyhose and disposable diapers are available.

Late 1960s–early 1970s   During the time of hippies and the women's liberation movement, many young women reject the bras and girdles their mothers wore. Some older women who had been influenced by the earlier suffragette movement are upset. For them, bras and girdles were a victory over corsets!

1980s–1990s	More and more underwear becomes outerwear: sports bras, slip dresses, camisoles, boxer shorts, tank tops, corsets worn as dress tops.
1990s	Body shaping depends more on excercise, diet, and plastic surgery than on the whalebone, steel, and elastic underwear of the past. The physical torso is sometimes called a "muscular corset."
Future	Scientists are working on underwear that will stay cleaner, drier, cooler, or warmer, depending on the climate. On the International Space Station, where there are no washers or dryers, astronauts may one day use bacteria to eat their used underwear!

FOR MORE INSIDE INFORMATION

For your own research it's fun to ask older family members and relatives what kinds of underwear they remember wearing. Local historical societies often have information on early underwear too.

www.fashion-era.com (clothing history, mostly English)

www.metmuseum.org (The Metropolitan Museum of Art in New York City has a good time line of art history on their website. It includes clothing and armor.)

Carter, Alison. *Underwear: The Fashion History*. New York: Drama Book Publishers, 1992.

Corey, Shana. *You Forgot Your Skirt, Amelia Bloomer!* New York: Scholastic Press, 2000.

Cunnington, C. Willett, and Phyllis Cunnington. *The History of Underclothes*. New York: Dover Publications, 1992. First published 1951 by Michael Joseph Ltd., London.

Eicher, Joanne B., Sandra Lee Evenson, and Hazel A. Lutz. *The Visible Self: Global Perspectives on Dress, Culture, and Society*. 2nd ed. New York: Fairchild Publications, 2000.

Ewing, Elizabeth. *Everyday Dress: 1650–1900*. New York: Chelsea House Publishers, 1984.

Farrell-Beck, Jane, and Colleen Gau. *Uplift: The Bra in America*. Philadelphia: University of Pennsylvania Press, 2002.

Steele, Valerie. *The Corset: A Cultural History*. New Haven: Yale University Press, 2001.

ACKNOWLEDGMENTS

The quote on page 25 is from *Lift Off! An Astronaut's Dream* by R. Mike Mullane. Originally published by Silver Burdett Press: 1994. Copyright 1994 R. Mike Mullane. Used by permission.

Blue Hill Public Library

The Carter Company

Charlotte Cushman

Chester County Historical Society

Cotton Inc.

DuPont

Goodwill Industries International, Inc.

Hadley Ferguson

Hagley Museum and Library

The Metropolitan Museum of Art

SMART (Secondary Materials and Recycled Textiles)